Symphony of Threads

Nizhal Kanda Nijangal

BY

Pugal *Yazhini*

Contents

"Nizhal Kanda Nijangal" can be translated as "Shadows Witnessing Realities" or "Realities Witnessed by Shadows."

The phrase suggests a connection between shadows and the observation or witnessing of truths or realities.

It might be used metaphorically to convey a deeper meaning, perhaps exploring themes of perception, hidden truths, or the interplay between light and darkness in understanding reality.

- **Nizhal (நிழல்):** This translates to "shadow" in English. It refers to the dark area produced by an object blocking the light.
- **Kanda (கண்ட):** This is the past tense of the verb "to see" in Tamil. It means "saw" or "witnessed."
- **Nijangal (நிஜங்கள்):** This translates to "realities" or "truths" in English. It signifies the state of being real or actual.

"Nizhal Kanda Nijangal" is a phrase in Tamil, a Dravidian language spoken predominantly in the Indian state of Tamil Nadu and in Sri Lanka.

Part 1: Facades of Reality

Chapter 1: Mirrored Messages

In the tranquil confines of her bathroom, Yazhini faced the mirror, its usual reflective surface now infused with an enigmatic glint. Today, it seemed more than a mere glass—it held secrets, whispers of truths waiting to be unveiled.

"Must be one of those peculiar mirror days," she mumbled with a half-smile, eyeing her own reflection as if expecting it to spill its clandestine knowledge. "Maybe I need more sleep."

To her surprise, the reflection seemed to shimmer in response, as if eager to share something beyond the ordinary.

"Sleep is overrated, my dear. There are greater mysteries to unravel," the mirror responded, leaving Yazhini momentarily caught between scepticism and curiosity.

"Okay, either I've finally lost it, or my mirror just spoke to me. Not sure which is more likely," she quipped, a smirk playing on her lips as she pondered the unusual interaction.

As the day unfolded, Yazhini stumbled upon a cryptic note concealed in her jacket pocket, its words weaving a narrative of shadows, secrets, and the intertwined fate of someone dear.

"The shadows dance with secrets, and Pugal's fate is entwined. Seek the café where echoes whisper."

"Spectacular. Whispers in cafés, secret notes—am I in a spy novel now? Pugal, if you're behind this, I hope there's a good reason," she remarked with a chuckle, the unfolding mystery laced with a touch of sarcasm.

Guided by curiosity, Yazhini found herself in a quaint café, its ambiance shrouded in a mysterious allure. With each sip of her coffee, the atmosphere seemed to thicken with anticipation. A stranger casually slipped into the seat opposite her, introducing himself as a bearer of hidden truths.

"Yazhini, your world is not what it seems. Pugal's fate is the first thread in a tapestry of hidden truths."

"Great, now strangers at cafés are philosophers. What's next, talking cats?" she quipped, a bemused smile lingering on her lips as she grappled with the surreal revelations.

The stranger handed Yazhini a small object, and as she examined it, the café's restroom mirror unexpectedly bore a message.

"The key you hold unlocks the echoes of forgotten realms. Embrace the unseen, Yazhini."

"Well, this just took a turn for the bizarre. Unseen realms? Do I get a map for those?" she wondered aloud, her words laced with a blend of amusement and intrigue.

Exiting the café, Yazhini inadvertently collided with a street performer dressed as a wizard, who pressed a tiny crystal ball into her hand.

"For your journey, brave seeker. The crystal reveals what the eyes cannot see."

"Oh, perfect! Just what I needed—a wizard and his crystal ball. Maybe I should've ordered tea instead," she mused, a smirk playing on her lips as she embraced the whimsical uncertainty of the day.

With the mysterious object and the crystal ball in hand, Yazhini continued her journey, the day unfolding into an unexpected blend of mystique and amusement.

Chapter 2: Threads of Destiny

As Yazhini stepped out of the café, the city embraced her with its usual hustle and bustle. The mysterious objects clutched in her hands seemed to radiate a quiet energy, as if beckoning her towards the unknown.

Amidst the city's cacophony, Yazhini's thoughts were a whirlwind of questions. She navigated the streets, weaving through crowds with the ease of someone both determined and curious.

"Unseen realms, forgotten echoes, and now a crystal ball. Is this some elaborate prank Pugal cooked up?" she mused, her steps echoing the rhythm of her contemplation.

The crystal ball nestled in her palm; Yazhini couldn't help but steal glances at it. It seemed to hold a universe of its own, a miniature galaxy encapsulated in a transparent orb. "Maybe I'll get a career change—Yazhini, the city's very own mystic detective. Beats the usual snooping around for clues," she chuckled to herself, embracing the absurdity of the situation.

In the distance, a clock tower tolled the hour, marking a moment of transition. Yazhini's destination loomed ahead—a nondescript building with an unassuming sign that read "Timeless Treasures."

As she entered the antique shop, a bell jingled overhead, announcing her arrival to an elderly man behind the counter. His eyes, however, held a glint of wisdom that transcended the years.

"Ah, Yazhini, seeker of hidden truths. I've been expecting you," he greeted, his words resonating with an uncanny certainty.

"Expecting me? Is this some sort of mystic hub?" she quipped, half-expecting the crystal ball to chime in with its own commentary.

The elderly man gestured towards an ancient-looking book on the counter, its pages weathered by time. "In the Chronicles of Ephemeral Echoes, destinies entwine like threads in a cosmic tapestry. You hold the key to unravelling their secrets."

Yazhini scanned the pages, each filled with cryptic symbols and passages that seemed to dance with hidden meanings. The room itself felt charged with an otherworldly energy.

"Chronicles of Ephemeral Echoes... fancier than your average detective novel title. Pugal, you sure know how to spice up a mystery," she remarked, a smirk playing on her lips.

The elderly man handed her a magnifying glass, encouraging her to scrutinize the book's intricacies. As Yazhini delved into the details, she realized the symbols weren't just random; they resonated with the enigmatic objects she now possessed.

"The crystal, the mirror, and now the book—all connected, Yazhini. The threads of destiny have chosen you to weave their tale," the elderly man spoke with a gravity that transcended the quaint surroundings.

With newfound determination, Yazhini set out to unravel the threads that intertwined her reality with echoes of forgotten realms. The city, once familiar, now held the promise of secrets waiting to be discovered.

As she exited the antique shop, the bell jingled once again, its sound echoing with the weight of ancient prophecies and unseen destinies. The journey had just begun, and Yazhini couldn't help but feel a mix of anticipation and amusement at the cosmic twists that lay ahead.

Chapter 3: Whispers in the Shadows

Yazhini traversed the city streets, the antique shop's revelations echoing in her thoughts. The enigmatic objects cradled in her hands seemed to pulse with an otherworldly energy, guiding her towards an unfolding mystery.

Passing through an alley shaded by ancient trees, Yazhini noticed shadows that seemed to dance to an unheard melody. The air grew thick with a sense of anticipation, and a voice, gentle yet insistent, whispered through the rustling leaves.

"Yazhini, seeker of echoes, the shadows have tales to share. Will you listen?"

She halted, her gaze shifting to the shadows that seemed to take on a life of their own. The crystal ball in her hand emitted a soft glow, casting patterns of light on the cobblestone path. "Alright, shadows, spill the secrets. I've got nowhere else to be," she quipped, half-expecting the trees to respond with laughter.

As if in response, the shadows began to weave a narrative—a tapestry of forgotten realms and intertwined destinies. Yazhini found herself drawn into a world where echoes whispered of love lost, of sacrifices made, and the dance of time that intertwined souls across dimensions.

"Love lost, sacrifices made... well, that's a poetic way to complicate things," she murmured, her mind a labyrinth of thoughts, each path leading to a new revelation.

The crystal ball, now held aloft, seemed attuned to the shadowy revelations. It refracted the ambient light, creating a kaleidoscope of images that blurred the lines between reality and the unseen realms.

"Guess I'm the chosen one, carrying a cosmic disco ball and all," Yazhini chuckled, finding humour in the surreal journey she had embarked upon.

As she continued through the alley, the shadows whispered not just of trials but also of triumphs, of destinies reshaped and unseen guardians watching over the threads of time.

A figure emerged from the shadows—an ethereal being with eyes that held the weight of centuries. They extended a hand towards Yazhini.

"Yazhini, seeker of echoes, the shadows acknowledge your presence. Embrace the unseen, for you are a guardian of threads yet untold."

"Guardian, huh? I always thought 'detective' had a nice ring to it, but I suppose guardian has a certain mystical flair," she remarked, accepting the hand that seemed to bridge the realms between the seen and the unseen.

As the figure dissipated into the shadows, leaving behind a trail of fading echoes, Yazhini pressed on. The city, now adorned with the soft glow of twilight, held the promise of more revelations. The crystal ball pulsed in her hand, a beacon guiding her towards a destiny intertwined with the cosmic dance of echoes and shadows.

The journey had only just begun, and Yazhini couldn't help but marvel at the unpredictable symphony playing out before her—an orchestration of threads that defied the confines of time and space.

Chapter 4: Threads Entwined, Echoes Unveiled

As Yazhini navigated the city's labyrinthine streets, the echoes of the mysterious alley lingered, like whispers carried by the evening breeze. The crystal ball she held emitted a soft glow, illuminating her path as if guided by an unseen force.

The city's heartbeat seemed to synchronize with the rhythm of her steps. Along the way, she encountered a street musician playing a haunting melody on a violin, each note resonating with the enigmatic energy that surrounded her.

"Music, shadows, and cosmic disco balls—seems like a party Pugal forgot to invite me to," she quipped, tossing a coin into the musician's case as a playful nod to the unfolding symphony of her journey.

The crystal ball responded to the music, refracting the melody into a visual kaleidoscope that danced in the air. The cityscape transformed into a canvas of ethereal patterns, blurring the lines between the tangible and the unseen.

Lost in the entrancing spectacle, Yazhini almost missed the subtle vibrations emanating from the crystal ball. As she focused, a quote surfaced in her mind, seemingly etched into the fabric of her thoughts:

In the dance of shadows, echoes become the threads that weave the tapestry of destinies.

"Ah, profound quotes—the hallmark of any self-respecting cosmic adventure," she mused, appreciating the cosmic irony of finding wisdom in the midst of the urban bustle.

Guided by the resonance of the crystal ball, Yazhini arrived at an old bookstore with a weathered sign that read "Whispers of Eternity." The door creaked open as she entered, greeted by the scent of aged parchment and the soft rustling of pages.

An elderly librarian, with eyes that seemed to hold the weight of stories untold, welcomed her.

"Yazhini, seeker of echoes, the whispers of eternity await you within these pages."

"More whispers? I hope they're at least offering coffee," she replied with a wry smile, appreciating the whimsy of the unfolding adventure.

The librarian led her to a section obscured by the shadows of towering bookshelves. In the dim light, ancient volumes revealed themselves, each bearing titles that hinted at the mysteries of time and echoes.

"Chronicles of Ephemeral Echoes, Threads Unravelled, Whispers Across Realms... Pugal, you've been holding out on me with your literary choices," Yazhini remarked, her fingers tracing the spines of the intriguing volumes.

As she delved into the pages, the crystal ball responded with a subtle glow, resonating with the ancient wisdom encapsulated within the words. The narratives spoke of guardians and seekers, of cosmic tapestries woven with threads of love, sacrifice, and the dance of echoes.

The librarian's voice, laden with a timeless wisdom, echoed through the hallowed space.

"In the words of forgotten scribes, destinies converge. The echoes you seek are threads entwined, waiting to be unravelled."

With newfound knowledge and a touch of humour, Yazhini left the bookstore, the crystal ball pulsing with a vibrancy that hinted at the next chapter of her journey.

The night embraced her with a celestial canopy, and as she ventured forth, she couldn't help but marvel at the interconnected threads that wove through the fabric of her existence—a cosmic tale where echoes whispered, and destiny unfolded in the dance of shadows and words.

Chapter 5: Veil of Reflections

Under the moonlit sky, Yazhini ventured into the heart of the city, her steps guided by the pulsating glow of the crystal ball. The nocturnal air carried a symphony of distant sounds—the rustle of leaves, the distant hum of traffic, and the muffled laughter from hidden corners.

As she approached an ancient fountain adorned with intricate carvings, Yazhini felt a subtle change in the atmosphere. The crystal ball responded, casting luminous ripples in the water.

"Water, reflections, and cosmic disco balls. What's next, a fish with life advice?" she quipped, bending down to examine the mesmerizing patterns on the fountain's surface.

To her surprise, the crystal ball revealed a reflection—a distorted yet familiar silhouette. Pugal's face seemed to emerge from the ripples, his eyes holding a silent message.

"Yazhini, unravel the threads, for within reflections lies the truth."

Her heartbeat quickened, and a determination welled within her. The fountain, once a mere landmark, now held the promise of revelations.

With the crystal ball held high, Yazhini stood in the midst of the water's gentle cascade. The reflections seemed to morph, merging the tangible cityscape with elusive shadows from realms beyond.

"Unravel the threads... easier said than done, Pugal," she murmured, focusing on the dancing reflections as if deciphering a cryptic code.

As she gazed into the crystal ball, a quote surfaced in her mind:

> *Reflections are not merely echoes of the past; they are doorways to unseen realms.*

The words resonated with the unfolding mystery, urging her to peer beyond the surface of the reflections. The fountain's waters shimmered with ethereal energy, revealing glimpses of parallel worlds and intertwining destinies.

A soft voice echoed from the depths of the reflections, carrying a melancholic yet hopeful melody.

"In the dance of reflections, where time intertwines, a guardian emerges, and echoes find their way home."

"Guardian, echoes, and a poetic fountain. This adventure needs a handbook," Yazhini remarked, a mixture of amusement and awe playing across her features.

With newfound insight, she left the fountain behind, the crystal ball still aglow with the secrets it held. The city, now drenched in the moon's silvery glow, seemed to embrace her journey with a silent acknowledgment.

As she walked through the winding streets, Yazhini couldn't shake the feeling that every step brought her closer to a truth woven within the threads of reflections—a truth waiting to be unveiled in the tapestry of cosmic echoes.

The night held its secrets, and Yazhini, guided by the luminous path of the crystal ball, pressed on, ready to unravel the veils that concealed the unseen realms reflected in the city's shadows.

Part 2: The Game Unfolds

Chapter 6: Echoes of Lies

Returning to the heart of the city, Yazhini found herself immersed in the labyrinth of skyscrapers and bustling streets. The crystal ball's glow persisted, its celestial radiance now blending seamlessly with the neon lights that adorned the urban landscape.

The pulsating energy led Yazhini to an inconspicuous door in the side alley of a skyscraper. As she approached, the door creaked open, revealing a dimly lit passage that seemed to extend into the depths of the building.

"Secret doors, hidden passages, and cosmic disco balls—I've officially become a character in an urban fantasy novel," she mused, her steps echoing in the narrow corridor.

The crystal ball, now held aloft, emitted a soft hum as Yazhini reached an unassuming elevator. Stepping inside, she noticed that there were no buttons, no floor numbers—only a strange symbol that matched those etched in the Chronicles.

As the elevator descended, a voice echoed through the confined space. “The game begins, Yazhini. Echoes of lies and truths intertwined, waiting for the seeker to unveil.”

“Game, lies, and truths. At least I’m not playing solitaire,” she quipped, the elevator’s descent seemingly synchronized with the unfolding mystery.

The doors opened to a dimly lit room adorned with an array of mirrors. In the centre stood a figure cloaked in shadows, their features obscured.

“You’ve entered the realm of mirrors, seeker. The reflections hold both deception and revelation,” the shadowy figure intoned.

“Deception and revelation in a room full of mirrors—sounds like my last family reunion,” Yazhini replied, her irreverent humour not lost in the cosmic game.

Each mirror reflected a different scene—a kaleidoscope of moments, some familiar, others entirely alien. Yazhini approached one that seemed to reveal Pugal engaged in a heated argument with an unknown figure.

"Echoes of lies, Pugal. What secrets are you keeping?" she murmured, her gaze fixed on the unfolding scenes.

The crystal ball, when directed towards the mirrors, revealed hidden messages within the reflections—cryptic symbols and whispered truths that danced on the edge of perception.

As Yazhini deciphered the messages, the room transformed. Mirrors shattered, and the shadowy figure dissipated into the cosmic echoes, leaving behind a trail of enigmatic laughter.

"The game unfolds, seeker. Seek the cipher that binds the lies and truths," echoed the disembodied voice.

"The cipher, huh? Let's hope it's not too cryptic," she quipped, a smirk playing on her lips as she left the room of mirrors, the crystal ball pulsating with a newfound intensity.

The city's nocturnal symphony accompanied Yazhini as she emerged into the night, the echoes of lies and truths intertwining in the cosmic dance. The game had begun, and she was determined to unravel its mysteries, one enigmatic revelation at a time.

Chapter 7: Whispers in the Ciphered Night

Exiting the room adorned with ancient tapestries, Yazhini found herself once again in the vibrant streets of the city. The crystal ball, now resonating with newfound energy, guided her towards an area where neon signs flickered in rhythmic patterns, creating a surreal atmosphere.

As she walked through the luminous streets, Yazhini noticed a subtle shift in the ambient sounds. Whispers of coded conversations floated in the air, and shadows seemed to gather around corners, hinting at hidden mysteries.

"A ciphered night, huh? Feels like I've stumbled into a spy thriller. Pugal, I hope you're enjoying the show," she quipped, her words punctuated by the enigmatic hum of the crystal ball.

The urban landscape transformed into a canvas of symbols and codes, each graffiti and sign bearing hidden messages. Yazhini felt like a detective in a cryptic noir, decoding the whispers of the city.

Approaching a clandestine door tucked away in an alley, Yazhini hesitated before entering. The crystal ball's glow intensified, urging her to unveil the secrets that lay within.

Behind the door, she found a dimly lit room adorned with vintage typewriters and computer screens. At the centre of the room sat a mysterious figure, fingers dancing over a keyboard.

"Welcome, seeker of echoes. The ciphered night reveals its encrypted truths," the figure spoke, their voice a melodic blend of secrecy.

"Encrypted truths? I was hoping for a straightforward crossword puzzle, but this works too," Yazhini remarked, her gaze shifting between the typewriters and screens.

The figure handed her a parchment with a series of cryptic symbols. "Decode the whispers of the ciphered night, and the path to revelation shall unfold."

As Yazhini delved into deciphering the symbols, the room seemed to pulse with an unseen energy. Each decoded message revealed fragments of a larger narrative—a tale of alliances and betrayals, of coded love letters and clandestine rendezvous.

"Ah, the city's secrets in binary code. Who knew urban life had its own encryption standard?" she mused, piecing together the puzzle with a blend of logic and intuition.

As the final symbol fell into place, the room's atmosphere shifted. Hidden panels opened, revealing a concealed passage that led further into the labyrinth of the ciphered night.

"The whispers acknowledge your mastery, seeker. Continue the dance through the ciphered echoes," declared the mysterious figure.

With the crystal ball in hand, Yazhini stepped into the secret passage, the glow now pulsating with the rhythm of the encrypted night. The city's nocturnal symphony played on, and she ventured forth, eager to unveil the next layer of the cosmic game—where shadows spoke in coded whispers, and each step was a dance through the enigma of the ciphered night.

Chapter 8: Enigma of the Labyrinth

Stepping back into the bustling city, Yazhini felt the weight of the unfolding game pressing upon her. The crystal ball pulsed with an insistent energy, urging her forward. Following its celestial glow, she found herself in the heart of a neon-lit district.

The streets seemed to twist and turn, forming a labyrinthine maze of colours and sounds. As Yazhini navigated the urban labyrinth, the crystal ball's glow intensified with each step, illuminating her path through the dazzling chaos.

"An urban maze? Pugal, you've really outdone yourself with this game of yours. I hope there's a prize at the end," she quipped, her voice carrying a mix of amusement and determination.

The crystal ball responded to her jest with a subtle shimmer, as if acknowledging the challenge that lay ahead. Yazhini pressed on, guided by the interplay of lights and shadows that danced on the city's walls.

Turning a corner, she entered an alley adorned with graffiti that seemed to come alive in the moonlight. The symbols and colours painted on the walls mirrored the cryptic messages she had uncovered in the room of mirrors.

"Artistic conspiracies, now that's a twist. Wonder if the graffiti artists are in on the cosmic secret," she pondered, running her fingers over the vibrant strokes.

As she traced the graffiti, the crystal ball projected shadows that coalesced into a mosaic of interconnected symbols. The alley itself seemed to morph, revealing hidden passages and doorways that defied the logic of the urban landscape.

"An enigma within an enigma. I suppose we're taking the scenic route in this labyrinth of yours, Pugal," she remarked, embracing the surreal nature of the unfolding game.

The crystal ball guided her through the labyrinth, its glow now leading to a nondescript door at the end of the alley. As Yazhini approached, the door swung open, revealing a dimly lit room adorned with ancient tapestries.

Seated in the centre was a figure shrouded in mystery—a guardian of the labyrinth. Their eyes bore the weight of cosmic secrets, and in their hands, they held a puzzle box adorned with the same symbols Yazhini had encountered throughout her journey.

"Seeker of threads, the labyrinth reveals its enigma. Solve the puzzle, unravel the cosmic dance," the guardian intoned.

"A cosmic puzzle boxes? Hope it comes with a manual," she quipped, eyeing the intricate symbols that adorned the enigmatic container.

As Yazhini began deciphering the puzzle, the room transformed. The ancient tapestries came to life, weaving a visual symphony that mirrored the celestial dance she had witnessed beneath the ancient tree.

The puzzle box, when unlocked, emitted a burst of cosmic energy, enveloping Yazhini in a momentary trance. Visions unfolded—of galaxies swirling, threads intertwining, and echoes resonating through the vastness of the cosmos.

"The labyrinth acknowledges your prowess, seeker. The game evolves, and the cosmic dance continues," declared the guardian.

With the puzzle solved, Yazhini left the room, the crystal ball now radiating with a transcendent luminosity. The city's maze awaited, and with each twist and turn, she couldn't help but marvel at the interconnected enigmas that painted her journey—an odyssey where urban landscapes and cosmic mysteries seamlessly intertwined.

Chapter 9: Shadows of Betrayal

Exiting the labyrinth, Yazhini found herself in a quieter part of the city, where the echoes of her footsteps reverberated against the hushed walls. The crystal ball's glow guided her towards a secluded park bathed in moonlight.

Beneath the ancient trees, shadows seemed to dance with an eerie rhythm. The air carried a sense of foreboding, and Yazhini couldn't shake the feeling that the game was about to take a darker turn.

"Shadows, moonlight, and a touch of drama. Pugal, you've really set the stage for this act," she mused, her senses heightened as she ventured deeper into the park.

The crystal ball, now pulsating with an ethereal intensity, led her to a forgotten gazebo. In its centre stood a figure, cloaked in darkness, their features veiled.

"Yazhini, seeker of echoes, the shadows harbour secrets of betrayal. Unravel the shadows, unveil the betrayer," the figure intoned, their voice echoing through the moonlit clearing.

"Betrayal? Now we're adding a touch of tragedy to the cosmic script," she remarked, a steely determination in her gaze as she focused on the enigmatic figure.

As Yazhini moved closer, the crystal ball projected shadows onto the gazebo's walls. Images unfolded—a web of deceit, clandestine meetings, and whispers that echoed with a sinister undercurrent.

"Shadows don't lie, Yazhini. Betrayal casts its silhouette, and the echoes bear witness," declared the figure, their eyes piercing through the darkness.

With each revelation, Yazhini felt the weight of betrayal weaving through the cosmic tapestry. The images coalesced into a mosaic of faces, and among them, Pugal's visage appeared, a mask of secrecy veiling his intentions.

"Pugal, what game are you playing?" she muttered, her thoughts a tumultuous sea of emotions as the shadows continued their haunting dance.

The crystal ball, when held aloft, revealed a cryptic message etched into the gazebo's stone floor—a riddle that hinted at the betrayer's motives and the next twist in the cosmic narrative.

"Betrayal's riddle, a puzzle within the shadows. Solve it, and the game unfolds further," urged the figure, their form dissipating into the night.

"Alright, shadows, betrayal, and a cosmic puzzle. This game just went from labyrinthine to labyrinth of emotions," she sighed, her gaze fixed on the enigmatic message.

As Yazhini contemplated the riddle, the park's shadows seemed to deepen, enveloping her in an aura of suspense. The crystal ball awaited its next revelation, and with determination in her heart, she delved into the intricacies of the cosmic enigma, ready to face the shadows and unveil the echoes of betrayal that lurked within.

Chapter 10: The Veiled Revelation

With the echoes of betrayal lingering in the moonlit park, Yazhini delved into the cryptic riddle etched into the gazebo's stone floor. The crystal ball in her hands responded to her contemplation, pulsating with an anticipation that matched the tension in the air.

As she deciphered the riddle, the shadows seemed to part, unveiling a hidden pathway leading deeper into the park. The crystal ball's glow intensified, guiding her towards an ancient well surrounded by willow trees—a well she hadn't noticed before.

"Well, well, well... what secrets do you hold?" she quipped, her voice cutting through the silence as she approached the enigmatic well.

The crystal ball, when held over the well, refracted the moonlight into a mesmerizing pattern, casting ripples across the water's surface. A soft, haunting melody emanated from the depths, and Yazhini felt a connection between the well and the cosmic tapestry she was unravelling.

As she peered into the well, visions unfolded—of veiled figures, concealed truths, and a revelation shrouded in mystery. The crystal ball projected images onto the willow trees, creating an ethereal tableau that mirrored the stories hidden within the well's waters.

"The well reveals the veiled truths, Yazhini. Seek the revelation, and the cosmic dance shall find its rhythm," whispered a disembodied voice, the very air resonating with the weight of untold secrets.

"Veiled truths, cosmic dance... Pugal, your narrative choices are getting quite poetic," she remarked, a wry smile playing on her lips as she embraced the surreal nature of the unfolding revelations.

Guided by the well's ethereal glow, Yazhini discovered a hidden passage beneath the willow trees. The crystal ball, now a beacon in the night, illuminated the pathway as she ventured deeper into the heart of the park.

The hidden passage led her to a secluded courtyard, bathed in starlight. In its centre stood a statue of a veiled dancer, frozen in a pose that seemed to capture the essence of cosmic grace.

"Veiled revelations in a cosmic ballet. This is turning into quite the celestial performance," she mused, her gaze fixed on the veiled dancer.

As Yazhini approached, the crystal ball resonated with the statue, projecting a series of symbols that mirrored the riddle she had deciphered. The veiled dancer seemed to come to life, the symbols swirling around her in a cosmic dance.

"The dance of veiled revelations, Yazhini. Decode the cosmic choreography, and the final act shall unfold," echoed the disembodied voice, the courtyard bathed in a celestial glow.

"Decoding cosmic choreography... now that's a challenge even for a seasoned dancer like me," she chuckled, her fingers tracing the symbols in the air as she sought to unravel the final layer of the cosmic mystery.

The courtyard embraced her in a symphony of starlight and shadows, and as Yazhini delved into the veiled revelations, she felt the threads of destiny pulling her towards the climax of the cosmic dance—a revelation that awaited its moment to be unveiled in the grand tapestry of "Nizhal Kanda Nijangal."

Part 3: The Weaver's Symphony

Chapter 11: Threads of Destiny Unravelled

In the starlit courtyard, Yazhini focused on decoding the cosmic choreography of symbols that swirled around the veiled dancer statue. The crystal ball responded to her efforts, projecting images and patterns that seemed to form a celestial language.

As she delved deeper into the cosmic dance, a surge of energy emanated from the symbols. The courtyard transformed, and Yazhini found herself surrounded by a celestial panorama—a tapestry of galaxies, constellations, and intertwining threads that spanned the vastness of space.

"Threads of destiny woven into the cosmic dance. This is beyond anything I could have imagined," she marvelled, her fingers gracefully tracing the patterns in the air.

The disembodied voice resonated through the starlit expanse, "Yazhini, seeker of threads, you have unravelled the cosmic choreography.

The time has come for the threads of destiny to reveal their ultimate secret."

With a burst of radiant energy, the veiled dancer statue transformed into a shimmering portal. The threads of destiny converged, creating a pathway that beckoned Yazhini into the cosmic unknown.

"Alright, cosmic portal, show me what lies beyond the veil," she said with a mix of excitement and anticipation, stepping through the radiant gateway.

On the other side, Yazhini found herself in a realm where time and space seemed to dance in harmony. Celestial beings, each a guardian of destiny, surrounded her. They spoke in harmonious whispers, revealing the intricacies of the cosmic tapestry.

"Yazhini, seeker of echoes, you stand at the threshold of the cosmic revelation. The threads of destiny converge in your hands," proclaimed the celestial beings, their voices resonating like celestial music.

Before her, a cosmic tapestry unfurled—an intricate weave of moments, choices, and interconnected destinies. Yazhini saw glimpses of her own life, entwined with the lives of others in a dance that transcended the boundaries of time.

"Destiny's tapestry, interwoven threads, and a dance that echoes through eternity. This is the grand finale," she whispered, awestruck by the cosmic spectacle.

As Yazhini reached out to touch the tapestry, the celestial beings bestowed upon her a crystal loom—a tool to weave and shape the threads of destiny. Each movement of her hands resonated through the cosmic tapestry, creating patterns that echoed across the universe.

"The weaver of destinies, Yazhini, the cosmic dance is now yours to guide," declared the celestial beings, their forms merging with the radiant energy of the cosmic realm.

With the crystal loom in hand, Yazhini felt the weight of cosmic responsibility. The threads of destiny responded to her touch, and as she began to weave, a new chapter unfolded—a chapter where echoes, destinies, and the cosmic dance were inextricably entwined.

As the celestial realm embraced her, Yazhini knew that her journey was not just a tale written in the stars but an ongoing symphony—a dance of threads and echoes that resonated through the cosmic expanse. And so, she continued to weave, shaping the destinies that echoed through the grand tapestry of "Nizhal Kanda Nijangal."

Chapter 12: Celestial Tapestry

In the aftermath of the revelation at the starlit courtyard, Yazhini stood at the nexus of the cosmic realm, her hands still adorned with the crystal loom. The celestial beings, embodiments of cosmic forces, surrounded her in a mesmerizing display of energy.

"Yazhini, weaver of destinies, you have glimpsed the intricate dance of threads that shape existence. The cosmic tapestry unfolds before you," intoned the celestial entities, their voices resonating like celestial music.

As Yazhini gazed upon the celestial tapestry, she saw the threads of countless lives interwoven in a breathtaking mosaic. Each thread told a unique story, from the smallest flutter of a butterfly's wing to the grand arcs of civilizations rising and falling.

"The cosmic tapestry, a chronicle of echoes, choices, and destinies entwined. It's both humbling and awe-inspiring," she whispered, a sense of reverence colouring her words.

The celestial beings guided Yazhini through the tapestry, revealing moments of joy, sorrow, love, and resilience. The threads of her own life were intertwined with others, creating a rich tableau of shared experiences.

“You are part of a vast and intricate design, Yazhini. Your choices send ripples through the tapestry, shaping the very fabric of existence,” conveyed the celestial entities.

Her thoughts turned to Pugal, and as if responding to her silent inquiry, a specific thread caught her attention—a thread veiled in shadows, its true nature concealed.

“Pugal’s thread, veiled and enigmatic. What secrets do you hold, my friend?” she pondered, her focus honing in on the mysterious twists within his destiny.

The celestial beings, sensing her curiosity, imparted cryptic insights. “Some threads are woven in the cosmic loom with purposeful ambiguity. The dance of shadows adds depth to the grand narrative.”

With newfound understanding, Yazhini continued to navigate the celestial tapestry. The crystal loom responded to her intent, allowing her to weave threads of hope, compassion, and understanding into the cosmic narrative.

As she wove, a profound realization dawned upon her—an awareness that every choice, every echo, contributed to the ever-evolving dance of existence. The cosmic tapestry, guided by the hands of the weaver, told a story that transcended time and space.

And so, surrounded by the celestial beings, Yazhini immersed herself in the harmonious choreography of the cosmic tapestry. The threads of destiny, both known and veiled, continued to unfold, creating a symphony of echoes that echoed through the vast expanse of the universe.

Chapter 13: Harmony of Echoes

In the celestial realm, Yazhini continued to weave the threads of destiny with the crystal loom bestowed upon her by the celestial beings. The cosmic tapestry responded to her touch, creating a symphony of patterns that echoed through the vast expanse.

As she explored this realm, Yazhini encountered celestial entities embodying different aspects of existence—beings of love, courage, wisdom, and more. Each entity contributed to the harmonious melody of the cosmic symphony.

“Harmony of echoes, where every thread tells a unique story. It’s like orchestrating the universe itself,” she marvelled, her fingers dancing gracefully with the crystal loom.

The celestial entities gathered around Yazhini, their energies intertwining with hers. They shared visions of worlds yet to be, destinies waiting to unfold, and the interconnectedness of all things in the grand cosmic dance.

"Yazhini, weaver of destinies, your role transcends the boundaries of time and space. The threads you weave echo through the tapestry of existence," spoke the celestial entities in unison.

Guided by their wisdom, Yazhini continued to shape the cosmic tapestry. She wove threads of compassion, courage, and understanding, creating patterns that radiated with profound meaning. As she delved deeper into the cosmic symphony, Yazhini discovered a thread that resonated with her own life—a thread that intertwined with the destinies of those she cared about, including Pugal.

"Pugal, your thread is woven into the cosmic dance. What mysteries does your destiny hold?" she pondered, her focus shifting to the threads that connected their lives.

The celestial entities sensed the complexity of Pugal's thread and offered cryptic insights. "In the dance of destinies, some threads are veiled in shadows. The echoes of choices made and paths untaken shape the cosmic narrative."

Determined to unravel the mysteries surrounding Pugal's destiny, Yazhini continued to weave, seeking clarity and understanding. The celestial realm responded with a kaleidoscope of visions, each revealing a facet of the intricate dance between their threads.

As the cosmic symphony played on, Yazhini felt a profound connection to the universe—a sense of purpose that went beyond her own existence. The threads of destiny, guided by her hands, echoed the beauty of life's interconnected tapestry.

And so, in the celestial realm, Yazhini embraced her role as the weaver of destinies, navigating the intricate dance of threads with grace and purpose. The cosmic symphony continued, harmonizing the echoes of existence in a transcendent melody.

Chapter 14: Echoes of Choices

Embraced by the celestial realm, Yazhini continued her journey as the weaver of destinies. The cosmic tapestry unfolded with every movement of her hands, each thread representing a life, a choice, an echo in the vast symphony of existence.

As she ventured deeper into the cosmic expanse, Yazhini encountered a nexus where threads converged and diverged—a place where echoes of pivotal choices resonated through the tapestry. The celestial beings accompanied her, their energies interwoven with the cosmic threads.

"Echoes of choices, Yazhini. Here, the threads reveal the impact of decisions made and the ripples they create across the tapestry," explained the celestial entities, their voices carrying the weight of collective wisdom.

Guided by their insight, Yazhini observed threads that shimmered with moments of profound decision-making. She witnessed the echo of a compassionate choice, a courageous stand, and the far-reaching consequences of seemingly trivial actions.

"These threads are like a cosmic reflection of every choice, a mirror to the consequences woven into the fabric of existence," she remarked, her eyes tracing the intricate patterns before her.

Amidst the celestial convergence, a specific thread caught her attention—the one that mirrored Pugal's choices, his journey entwined with shadows and enigma.

"Pugal's echoes, his choices resonate through the cosmic dance. What paths have you walked, my friend?" Yazhini pondered, her focus narrowing on the enigmatic twists within his thread.

The celestial beings, recognizing her quest for understanding, granted glimpses into the pivotal moments of Pugal's life. Each vision revealed a crossroads where choices shaped his destiny—some bathed in light, others veiled in shadows.

As Yazhini delved deeper into the echoes of Pugal's choices, she discovered a nexus where his thread intersected with hers—a moment that held the potential to unravel the mysteries surrounding their intertwined destinies.

"Choices entwined; destinies converged. The dance of echoes continues, Yazhini. The cosmic tapestry awaits your touch," conveyed the celestial entities, their ethereal forms resonating with cosmic energy.

With newfound clarity, Yazhini resumed her role as the weaver of destinies. The crystal loom responded to her intent, allowing her to shape the echoes of choices with purpose and insight. As she wove, Yazhini felt the threads of destiny resonate with the harmonious rhythm of the celestial realm.

The echoes of choices, both known and veiled, contributed to the grand symphony that echoed through the cosmic expanse—a testament to the interconnectedness of all life and the profound impact of every decision made along the journey of existence.

Chapter 15: Threads of Eternity

In the cosmic nexus where echoes of choices intertwined, Yazhini felt a profound connection to the threads of destiny, especially the enigmatic path woven by Pugal. As she delved into the nexus, guided by the celestial entities, the tapestry revealed a pivotal moment—a convergence of their destinies.

Before her eyes, the threads of Yazhini and Pugal merged in a celestial dance. The crystal loom responded with a radiant glow, resonating with the cosmic energy that surged through their interconnected destinies.

"Pugal's choices echo in harmony with yours, Yazhini. The threads of eternity converge, revealing a tapestry that transcends the boundaries of time," intoned the celestial entities, their forms shimmering with celestial light.

As the cosmic tapestry unveiled the moment of convergence, Yazhini witnessed a revelation—a twist that added a new layer of meaning to their intertwined destinies. Pugal's enigmatic choices were not merely a product of circumstance but a deliberate dance orchestrated by cosmic forces.

"Pugal, you and I are threads in a grand design, part of a cosmic narrative that extends beyond our understanding," she whispered, her heart resonating with a profound realization.

The celestial beings bestowed upon Yazhini a final vision—an image of a cosmic loom, a loom that transcended the confines of the celestial realm. It represented the collective weaving of destinies by individuals across the vast cosmic tapestry.

"Threads of eternity, Yazhini. The cosmic loom awaits the touch of every seeker, every weaver of destinies. The dance of echoes continues through the hands of those who shape the tapestry," conveyed the celestial entities, their voices carrying the weight of cosmic wisdom.

As the vision unfolded, Yazhini found herself back in the city, the crystal loom in her hands glowing with a transcendent luminosity.

The echoes of choices, the dance of destinies, and the threads of eternity resonated within her.

With a sense of purpose and newfound awareness, Yazhini embraced her role as a weaver of destinies. The cosmic loom extended beyond her, inviting others to join in the grand dance of existence.

The final twist lay not in a singular revelation but in the realization that every individual, every choice, contributed to the ever-unfolding cosmic narrative. The story of "Nizhal Kanda Nijangal" was not merely a tale with a definitive ending; it was an ongoing symphony—a dance of threads and echoes that transcended the boundaries of time and space.

And so, Yazhini, with the crystal loom in hand, continued to weave the threads of eternity, shaping the cosmic tapestry with each choice and echo.

The celestial entities watched in silent approval, their energies merging with the vibrant cosmic dance that echoed through the vast expanse of existence—a dance that would continue for eternity.

In the grand story of life, the chapters are filled not just with moments but with the choices that define our narrative

The End

Life is a cosmic symphony, where each choice adds a note to the grand composition of our existence.—Celestial Wisdom

---

Eternal Echoes

As Yazhini continued to weave the threads of destiny, an unexpected resonance echoed through the cosmic tapestry. The celestial beings, guardians of the celestial realm, shared a revelation that transcended time itself.

"Yazhini, seeker of threads, the cosmic dance holds an eternal secret. The threads of existence loop and intertwine, creating echoes that transcend the boundaries of past, present, and future," conveyed the celestial entities, their voices carrying a mysterious undertone.

With a profound sense of anticipation, Yazhini focused on a specific thread within the celestial tapestry—the one that seemed to echo beyond the confines of linear time. As she wove, the boundaries between moments blurred, and a revelation unfolded.

Pugal's thread, veiled in shadows and enigma, revealed a connection that defied the conventional flow of time. A realization dawned upon Yazhini—the echoes of choices made were not confined to a singular timeline. Instead, they created a continuous loop, influencing past, present, and future in an eternal dance.

In a surprising twist, Yazhini discovered that the threads of destiny were not merely linear but formed an infinite spiral, intertwining the echoes of choices in a timeless symphony. The cosmic tapestry, once perceived as a linear narrative, now revealed itself as an eternal echo, where every choice resonated through the vast expanse of existence.

As Yazhini embraced this revelation, the celestial beings bestowed upon her the wisdom of eternal echoes—an understanding that transcended the limitations of temporal boundaries. The cosmic dance, she realized, was a perpetual symphony, weaving threads of destiny in an eternal echo that reverberated through the fabric of time itself.

And so, with the newfound knowledge of eternal echoes, Yazhini continued to weave the cosmic tapestry, guiding the threads of existence in a dance that spanned the infinite expanse of eternity. The story concluded with a sense of continuity, a seamless loop of destiny, and the eternal beauty of choices echoing through the timeless corridors of the celestial realm.

Life is a canvas, and with each day, we paint strokes of laughter, hues of resilience, and shades of endless possibilities—Pugal Yazhini

---

****

Pugal ***Yazhini***

****

Life is a **Journey**

THE END

Love and **Live**

www.ingramcontent.com/pod-product-compliance
Lightning Source LLC
LaVergne TN
LVHW022028200926
848481LV00007B/2584
9798227042705